Cock -A- Doodle Moooo!

A Mixed-Up Menagerie

Keith DuQuette

G. P. Putnam's Sons

In ancient times, stories were told
of wondrous beasts, strange to behold.
Many of these mythic creatures
combined different animal features.

Griffin
(Lion + Eagle)

It would go to any measure
just to guard its golden treasure.

Kappa
(Monkey + Tortoise)

A people-eating river spirit—
little children learned to fear it!

Hippocampus
(Horse + Dolphin)

This proud creature was said to be ridden by the god of the sea.

Cockatrice
(Rooster + Serpent)

A monster with poisoned breath.
One look at him meant certain death!

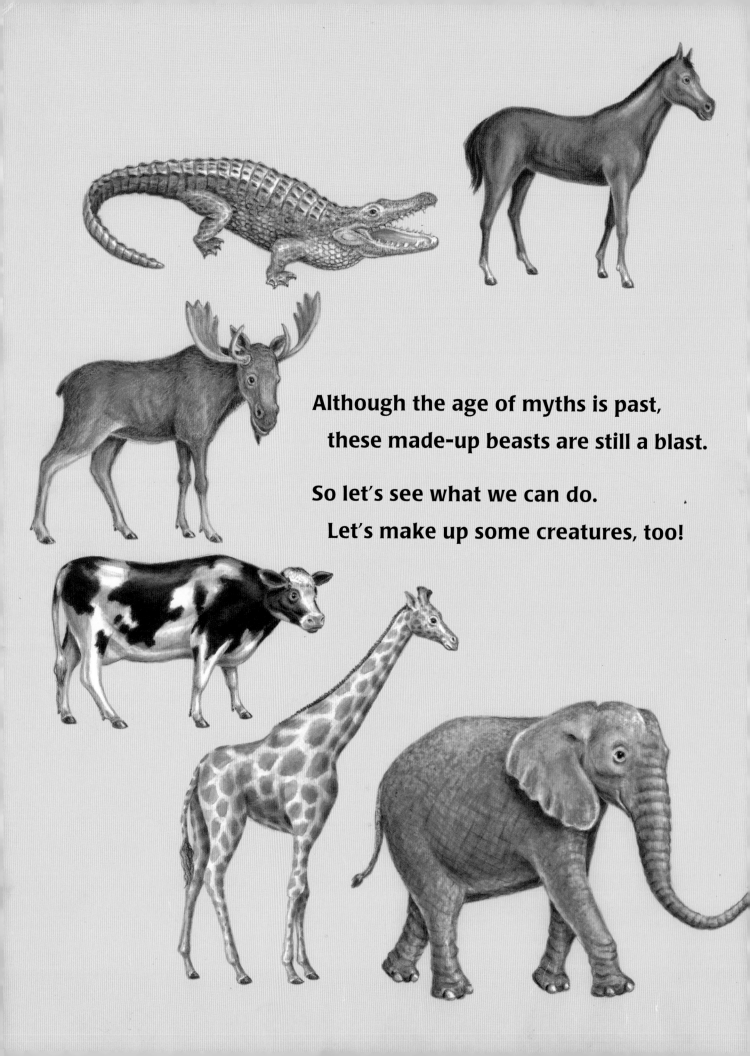

Although the age of myths is past,
    these made-up beasts are still a blast.

So let's see what we can do.
    Let's make up some creatures, too!

Imagine the possibilities!

The endless curiosities . . .

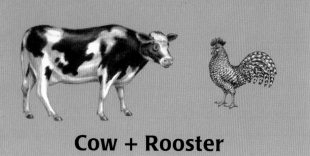

Cow + Rooster

Cooster

Imagine your surprise at dawn
to be roused by a cooster's call—
"Cock-a-doodle moOOO,
I've got milk for you."

Parrot + Gorilla

Parilla

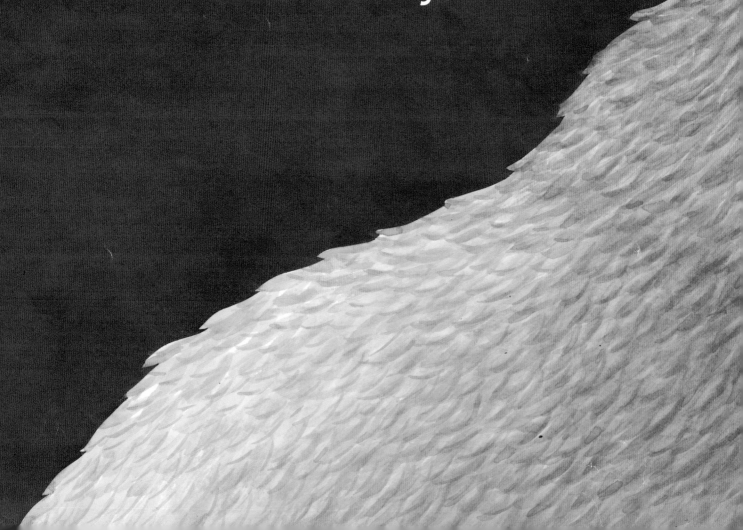

"Parilla wants a banana."

"Parilla wants a bunch."

And then he wants your breakfast,

and then he wants your lunch!

Giraffe + Tarantula

Girantula

If you ever chance to see
it slowly creeping up a tree,
my advice is—
let it be.

Hog + Grasshopper

Hoghopper

Hoghopper.
Big bopper.
Belly flopper!

Snail + Horse

Snorse

The snorse races
at **molasses** paces.
Inching forward in a pack,
it takes three days to round the track.

Mosquito + Elephant

Mosquiphant

Beware of the giant mosquiphant!
Its stinging trunk will leave a lump
that's bigger than your head!

But don't you worry, don't you cry,
a mosquiphant's too **fat** to fly.

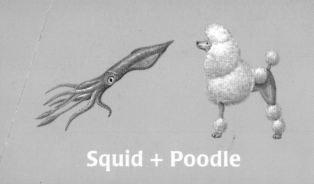

Squid + Poodle

Squoodle

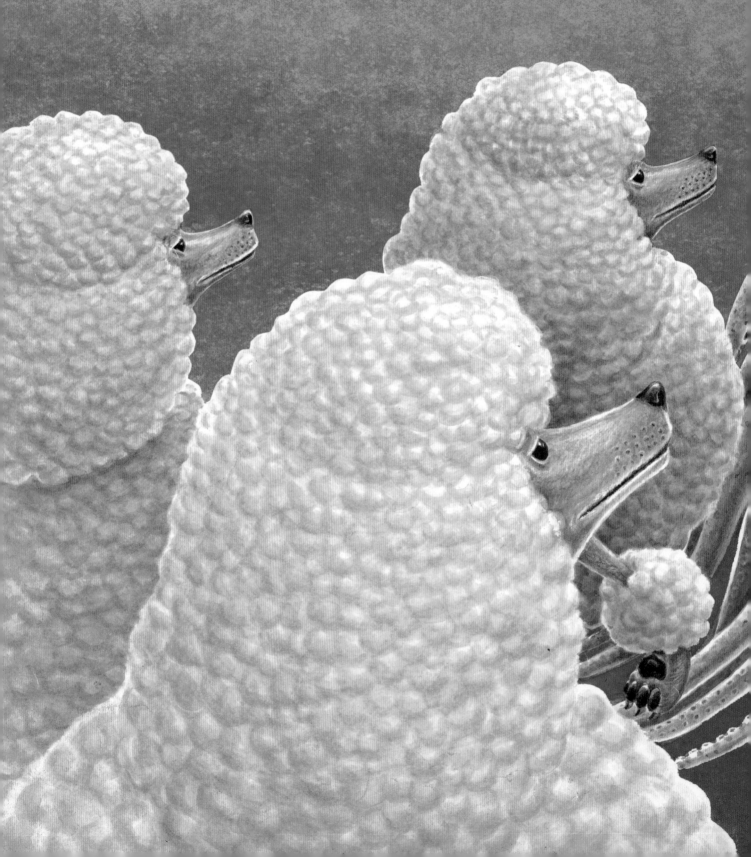

Oodles of squoodles swimming so free,
fluffy and lovely queens of the sea.
But what in the world is a squoodle to do
with all of this water . . .

and no shampoo?

Frutterfly

I think I saw a frutterfly.

Yes, I saw him flutter by.

And do you know just what he spoke?

A very fluent "C r o a k, c r o a k, c r o a k !"

Tortoise + Hare

Tortare

Once upon a time,
   the tortoise beat the hare.
Now, as a tortare,
   they're winning as a pair.

Mouse + Crocodile

Mouscodile

Not your average timid mouse,

he's moving freely through the house.

Sassy, bold and getting fat,

he skipped the cheese and ate **the cat!**

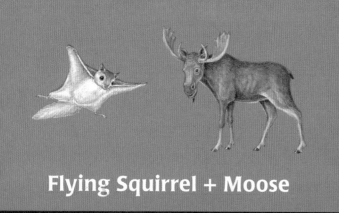

Flying Squirrel + Moose

Flying Squoose

When a *flying* squoose
is on the loose,
can oak and spruce
take the abuse?

Firefly + Pigeon

Firefligeon

A flock of firefligeons
c o o i n g in the dark.
Each and every night,
a light show in the park.

**Of all the animals we could combine,
what kind of creatures would *you* design?**

Let your imagination run free.
Create your own menagerie.

Imagine the possibilities!
The endless curiosities . . .

Here are some animal combinations found in myths and legends from around the world:

Ammut ➤ Part crocodile, lion and hippopotamus. This monster was known as the "Eater of the Dead." She lived in the Underworld, crouching beside a lake of fire. (Egyptian)

Baku ➤ Part lion, horse, tiger and cow. This good spirit, often called the "Eater of Dreams," eats a person's bad dreams, making them harmless or even good luck. (Japanese)

Capricorn ➤ A fish-tailed goat. This tenth sign of the zodiac symbolizes the powerful energy of the earth and the water. (Babylonian)

Chimera ➤ Part lion, goat and snake. This female monster is often shown as a three-headed beast with a flame-throwing goat's head rising from the middle of her back. (Greek)

Cockatrice ➤ Part rooster and snake. One glance into the eye of this hideous beast would mean a certain death. Its poison breath could wither the mightiest tree or shatter the largest stone. Also known as the Basilisk. (Greek/Roman)

Dog of Fo ➤ The little lion-dog. It combined the power of a lion and the loyalty of a dog. It is often shown with a paw resting on a ball—thought to be the Pearl of Wisdom. (Chinese)

Feng-Huang ➤ Part pheasant and peacock.
King of the feathered race, it is a symbol of peace and everlasting love. (Chinese)

Griffin ➤ Part lion and eagle. This master of the earth and sky combined strength and intelligence. It was said to build a nest of gold, which it fiercely guarded. (Middle Eastern/Greek)

Hippocampus ➤ Half horse and dolphin. This powerful swimming creature was often ridden by the god of the sea or shown in teams pulling his great chariot. (Greek/Roman)

Kappa ➤ Part tortoise and monkey. This man-eating river spirit was surprisingly polite. He loved to eat cucumbers. People would write the names of their family on cucumbers and throw them into the water to please the Kappa. This would keep their loved ones from his clutches. (Japanese)

Questing beast ➤ Part snake, leopard, lion and deer. In the tales of King Arthur, this secretive and speedy creature was hunted but never captured. It was said to make a tremendous noise from its belly, like the sound of forty angry dogs howling and growling at once. (British)

Quetzalcoatl ➤ Part bird and snake. Known as the "Plumed Serpent," it represented the earth and sky and was a very powerful symbol of rebirth. (Toltec/Aztec)

To Virginia

Special thanks to John Rudolph.

Library of Congress Cataloging-in-Publication Data
Du Quette, Keith. Cock-a-doodle moooo! : a mixed-up menagerie / Keith DuQuette.
p. cm. Summary: Short rhymes describe mythical animals as well as new animal hybrids. Includes a short
glossary of mythical animal terms. [1. Imaginary creatures—Fiction. 2. Animals, Mythical—Fiction.
3. Stories in rhyme.] I. Title. PZ8.3.D935Co 2004 [E]—dc21 2003008516 ISBN 0-399-23889-1
1 3 5 7 9 10 8 6 4 2
First Impression